Millie Finds a Feather

Written by
Judith Ellis

Illustrated by
Rebeckah Griffiths

ISBN: 978-1-913662-23-3

First published 2021
by Rowanvale Books Ltd
The Gate
Keppoch Street
Roath
Cardiff
CF24 3JW
www.rowanvalebooks.com
Library Cataloguing in Publication Data.
A catalogue record for this book is available from the British Library.

In memory of my lovely Dad,
who thought I couldn't see him feeding Millie all the biscuits.

Millie the black and white Border Collie puppy trotted off to find her friends Holly and Molly.

Holly was a white rabbit with one black ear.

Molly was a little grey rabbit with a white, fluffy tail.

"Hello, Millie," said Molly. "Do you know there is a feather on your nose?"

"Yes," said Millie. "It won't come off."

"I will get it off for you," said Molly.

So with her round, fluffy, white bunny tail, Molly wiggled and squiggled on Millie's nose, but the feather would not come off.

"Let me try to get it off for you," said Holly.

Holly wiggled and squiggled her long, thin bunny ears on Millie's nose, but the feather would not come off.

"What's going on here then?" said a little voice. It was Fuzzy the long-haired black and brown guinea pig.

He saw the feather. "I can get that off for you," he said.

So with his long, fuzzy fur, he wiggled and squiggled on Millie's nose, but still the feather would not come off.

Then along came Buttons the little brown hamster.

"Let me try. I can get it off for you," said Buttons, in a very squeaky voice.

So Buttons climbed onto Millie's tail, scurried along her back and sat on her head, but he simply could not reach the feather.

"This is just no good at all," said Millie, in a very sad voice.

"Don't be sad," said Fuzzy. "We all still think you are the prettiest dog ever, even with a feather stuck to your nose."

Buttons, Holly and Molly all tried to cheer Millie up as well.

Holly sang Millie a little song, but that didn't work.

Molly did a little dance, but that didn't work.

Buttons did a little song and a dance, but that didn't work either.

Bob Robin had been looking down from his tree, watching everything that was going on.

Millie was feeling very sorry for herself by now and was lying down with her head on her paws.

Bob Robin flew down from the tree and landed right on Millie's head.

"I can get the feather off your nose," he said.

"No, you can't," said Millie sadly. "Nobody can."

Bob Robin puffed up his bright red chest, flapped his wings and landed on Millie's nose.

"Now you have Bob Robin *and* a feather on your nose," laughed Holly.

Bob Robin started to pull at the feather with his beak. First this way, then that way, but it just would not come off.

"I told you," said Millie, sounding even sadder.

"Gosh," said Bob Robin. "That was hard. You are right—it just won't come off."

Suddenly, the garden gate opened and in came Maisy, Millie's owner.

"Come here, Millie," said Maisy. "You have a feather on your nose."

"Yes, I know," said Millie. "It just won't come off."

Maisy took a deep breath and then she blew, but the feather would not come off.

Holly, Molly, Buttons, Fuzzy and Bob Robin all watched as Maisy took another deep breath.

Maisy blew and she blew and she blew, until finally she blew the feather right off Millie's nose.

"There! It's gone," she said.

Millie was so happy she began to bark loudly and run around the garden wagging her tail.

Maisy picked the feather up and put it in her pocket, just in case there was a puff of wind and it landed on Millie's nose again.

All the animals were happy for Millie.

It had been a very busy day for them all.

Bob Robin flew back to his nest.

Molly and Holly went back to their hutch.

Buttons ran very quickly back to his little cage.

And Fuzzy stayed in the garden and fell asleep in the long grass.

Millie was also very tired, so she snuggled into her bed and fell fast asleep, happy that the feather was no longer stuck on her nose.

Author Profile

I live in Swansea, South Wales and have recently retired, which has given me the time to write *Millie Finds a Feather.*

Millie has been part of our family for fourteen years, since she arrived one Christmas Eve when she was just nine weeks old.

I love walking, and as Swansea has the most wonderful coastline (though not such wonderful weather!), Millie and I have spent many an hour enjoying the views.

I also have a passion for photography, which has probably resulted in Millie being the most photographed dog in Wales. In fact, I'm sure I have more photos of Millie than I do of my daughters—I think both girls would agree to that!

Millie has been a huge part of our family life, along with a constant flow of small furry animals. The rabbits, guinea pig and hamster in this story are just a few of the animals we have enjoyed as a family while my daughters were growing up. The personality and comical behaviour of each animal inspired me to write *Millie Finds a Feather.*

This is the first in a series of *Millie Finds* books.

***

What Did You Think of *Millie Finds a Feather?*

A big thank you for purchasing this book. It means a lot that you chose this book specifically from such a wide range on offer. I do hope you enjoyed it.

Book reviews are incredibly important for an author. All feedback helps them improve their writing for future projects and for developing this edition. If you are able to spare a few minutes to post a review on Amazon, that would be much appreciated.

Publisher Information

Rowanvale Books provides publishing services to independent authors, writers and poets all over the globe. We deliver a personal, honest and efficient service that allows authors to see their work published, while remaining in control of the process and retaining their creativity. By making publishing services available to authors in a cost-effective and ethical way, we at Rowanvale Books hope to ensure that the local, national and international community benefits from a steady stream of good quality literature.

For more information about us, our authors or our publications, please get in touch.
www.rowanvalebooks.com
info@rowanvalebooks.com

CPSIA information can be obtained
at www.ICGtesting.com
Printed in the USA
LVHW071633100521
687012LV00001B/7